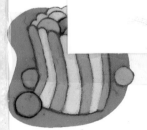

And gobstoppers.

Goblin Babies
They eat *anything*.

Kaye Umansky
GOBLINZ!

illustrated by Andi Good

PUFFIN BOOKS

PUFFIN BOOKS

Published by the Penguin Group
Penguin Books Ltd, 80 Strand, London WC2R 0RL, England
Penguin Putnam Inc., 375 Hudson Street, New York, New York 10014, USA
Penguin Books Australia Ltd, 250 Camberwell Road, Camberwell, Victoria 3124, Australia
Penguin Books Canada Ltd, 10 Alcorn Avenue, Toronto, Ontario, Canada M4V 3B2
Penguin Books India (P) Ltd, 11 Community Centre, Panchsheel Park, New Delhi – 110 017, India
Penguin Books (NZ) Ltd, Cnr Rosedale and Airborne Roads, Albany, Auckland, New Zealand
Penguin Books (South Africa) (Pty) Ltd, 24 Sturdee Avenue, Rosebank 2196, South Africa

Penguin Books Ltd, Registered Offices: 80 Strand, London WC2R 0RL, England

www.penguin.com

First published in Puffin Books 2002
1 3 5 7 9 10 8 6 4 2

Text copyright © Kaye Umansky, 2002
Illustrations copyright © Andi Good, 2002
All rights reserved

The moral right of the author and illustrator has been asserted

Printed in Hong Kong by Midas Printing Ltd

Except in the United States of America, this book is sold subject to the condition that it shall not, by
way of trade or otherwise, be lent, re-sold, hired out, or otherwise circulated without the publisher's
prior consent in any form of binding or cover other than that in which it is published and without a
similar condition including this condition being imposed on the subsequent purchaser

British Library Cataloguing in Publication Data
A CIP catalogue record for this book is available from the British Library

ISBN 0-141-31329-3

Contents

1. Shy

S hy the Goblin came walking
down the lane in his best shoes.
Although the sun was shining, he wore
a big coat, mittens and a huge scarf.
His hat was pulled well down. His
mum always made him wrap up well,

in case he caught cold.

As usual, Shy was thinking.
Thinking isn't a Goblin Thing, but
Shy was doing it anyway. He
always thought the same things.
About how great it would be to have
a friend. Even better, friends. Maybe,
just maybe, even belong to a Gaggle!

he had to undo his top button.

"*Vrrrmmm*," revved Wheels. "I'm Wheels. That's Twinge and his little brother Grizzle."

"He's eating twigs," said Shy wonderingly.

"Yeah," said Twinge. "He does that. He's just a baby."

"Boo *hoooooo* ..."

"Sorry, sorry, didn't mean it. Eat your twigs."

Tuf sat down and began to haul
his boots off.

"So," he said to Shy. "You comin'
in or what?"

"All right," said Shy, after a
moment's pause. Everyone watched
as he unwound his scarf and hung it
carefully on a branch. Then he
removed his coat, revealing a thick
green jumper. He took that off as well.
Underneath was a thick blue one.

Under *that* was a yellow one. Finally,
he got down to his vest. He folded all
his jumpers, placed them in a neat
pile and began to take his shoes off.

"Ready?" said Oggy. "You can
have a go with my bucket, if you like."

So Shy stepped into the muddy pond. Mud squished up between his toes. It was great!

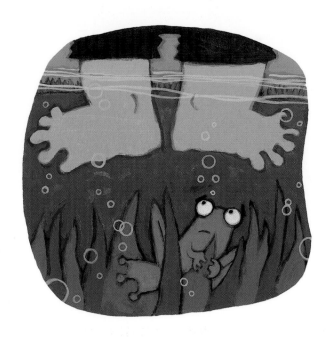

3. The Gaggle

S ome time later, muddy and
happy, they all sat beneath the
tree, looking at the pile of interesting
things they had found in the muddy
pond.

"Lots of tins," said Twinge. "And the old boot's good. And the bottle might come in useful for something."

"No frogs though," sighed Wheels. "*Vrrrmm.*"

"Still," said Shy. "It was the best fun I've ever had."

Everyone stared at him.

"We always have fun like this," said Oggy.

"Not me. But this was good.
Almost like being in a Gaggle."

"You need seven for a Gaggle,"
said Wheels.

They all stared at each other.

"How many are we?" asked Tuf.

"Six," said Shy promptly.

"Wow!" admired Tuf. "You're
good."

"It's not enough though," said Shy.

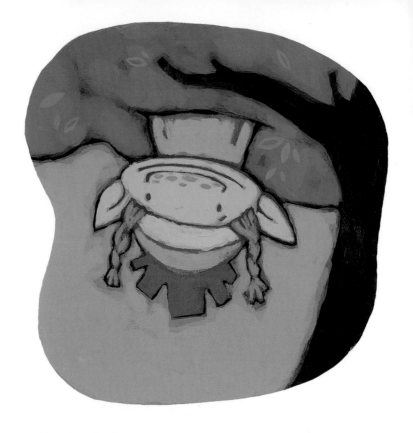

"Wheels is right. It has to be seven."

"How many more is dat?" asked
Tuf hopelessly.

"One," said a voice from above.
There was a rustling noise. The leaves
parted, and an upside-down head
with pigtails appeared.

"Huh!" said Oggy. "It's Cloreen Gobbles. Go away."

"Why?" enquired Cloreen, swinging down. "Can I be in your Gaggle? I've got gobblegum."

She blew a big, pink bubble and produced a bag from her pocket. That was the best thing about Cloreen. Her mum owned a sweet shop.

"No," said Oggy scornfully. "We don't want an old *girl*."

Cloreen blew another bubble and said, "I know where there's a shed. It could be our Club House."

"Hah!" scoffed Oggy. "Dream on!"

"I don't know," said Shy excitedly. "A Club House would be good, wouldn't it?"

A little silence fell. "At least we can *look*." Hopefully, he asked Tuf, "Can't we?"

"Yeah," said Tuf, eyeing Cloreen's bag. "We can *look*."

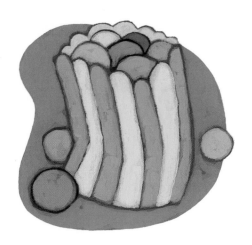

4. The Club House

The shed was dark and dirty. There were upturned buckets and big tins and sacks of coal to sit on. It was just right for a Club House.

"Can we have a password?" begged Shy as they peered in. "Please, oh please!"

Everyone wanted to know what a password was. Shy explained that it was a special word you said at the door.

"I know a special word," said Tuf. "Sausages."

"*Vrmmmm!* Let's try it!" revved Wheels excitedly.

So they all went in, muttering "Sausages!" in a mysterious way.

"That was good," giggled Cloreen, sitting on a sack next to Oggy. "It's fun being in a Gaggle, isn't it, Oggy?"

"Go away, Cloreen," growled Oggy, moving to a bucket.

For a while,
they just sat
around in the
gloom, popping
bubbles.
Grizzle wasn't allowed
gobblegum because he
got tangled in it, so he
ate coal.

"Now what?" said Oggy, over the chewing, popping and crunching noises.

"Can we have a secret sign?" begged Shy. This was all so new and exciting, he could hardly breathe. He had made six new friends. He had taken off his clothes, down by the muddy pond. Just like that! And he hadn't even caught cold yet!

"Like what?" asked Oggy.

"Like, hold up our thumbs."

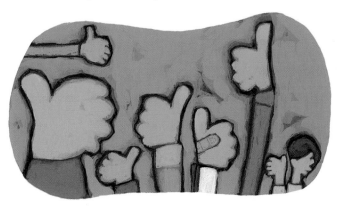

"How many?" asked Tuf. If it was more than three, he was in deep trouble.

Shy saw his anxious expression and added, "Or we can keep it simple and pull on our ears."

"I like it," said Tuf, relieved. Even *he* couldn't get that wrong.

"We need a name too" said Shy, quite carried away. "Any ideas?"

Blank faces all round.

"Sausages?" ventured Tuf, after a while. Well, it had worked the first time.

"It's *good*," said Shy loyally. "But not quite right."

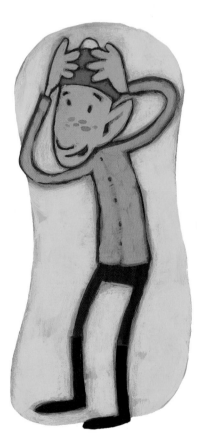

"Goblins With Hats On?" suggested Twinge.

"Ye-eesss. Although all Goblins have got hats on.

We need something a bit more
special. I was thinking ..." Shy
hesitated.

"What?" chorused everyone.

"Well – it's probably no good,
but ..."

"What?"

"The Goblineers."

"Oh, *I* get it," said Cloreen, after a short silence. "We pull our Goblin *ears* when we make the secret sign. Clever!"

To Shy's delight, everyone thought this was an excellent name.

"Is that it?" asked Oggy. "Are we a Gaggle now?"

"Yes," said Shy happily. "We are."

"So what do we do now then?" Wheels wanted to know.

"We could tidy our Club House," suggested Cloreen. "We could make curtains and ..." She caught sight of their faces and added brightly, "Anyone want the last gobblegum?"

"We don't want to do *that*," said Oggy, quickly taking it. "There must be something better to do than *that*."

"I think we should do good deeds," said Shy. Everyone stared. He went a bit red.

"Like what?" asked Wheels.

"Like – odd jobs."

"I know an odd job," said Tuf. "Puttin' toothpaste in tubes. Dat's odd."

"I was thinking more of cleaning or gardening. Or helping old ladies over the road. Three good deeds a day."

"Oh dear," sighed Tuf. "More numbers."

"Goblins don't do good deeds," said Twinge.

"So we could be different. We could, couldn't we?" Shy stared hopefully at Tuf.

"I suppose we could give it a go," said Tuf. "But I'll need help wid de maths."

5. The Witch

"Yes?" squawked a shrill voice from behind the door of a tumbledown hovel. "Who is it?"

"Us," said Tuf. "De Goblineers. Need any jobs doin', missus?"

There came the noise of rattling chains and bolts being drawn. The door opened, and Old Ma Musty's frizzy grey head poked out. She wore an old dressing gown, shabby slippers and a cross expression.

"What?" she snapped.

"We is de Goblineers," explained Tuf patiently. "Come to do you a good deed."

"You mad or something?"

"No. Just – helpful."

"Hmm. Well, I suppose the kitchen could do with a tidy. You'd better come in."

The kitchen needed more than a tidy. The sink was a mountain of greasy dishes. Cobwebs hung from the rafters and the floor was a disgrace. Grizzle made for the overflowing bin, sensing exciting food opportunities.

"I'll leave you to it then," said Old Ma Musty. "Me, I'm going back to bed for some shut-eye. I was up all night capering under the moon. Done something to my back."

The Goblineers stared around the horrible kitchen as her footsteps shuffled away.

"Anyone know how to clean?" asked Tuf.

Nobody did.

Some while later, they sat in glum silence in the Club House. Shy was trying to brush soot stains from his coat. Tuf had scorch marks on the seat of his trousers. Wheels had a dent in his helmet. Oggy was attempting to remove his bucket from his head. Cloreen was staring sadly

at her singed hat. Twinge had a lump
on his head where a broomstick had
hit him and Grizzle was asleep with a
mouth full of potato peelings.

"Wasn't much of a success, was
it?" sighed Twinge. "Our first good
deed."

"I still say you shouldn't have
thrown those jars away, Cloreen,"
said Oggy, from inside the bucket.
"That's what really made her mad."

"How was I to know they were full of magic herbs?" said Cloreen. "Anyway, you made the flood."

"An' I started the fire," confessed Tuf unhappily. "I didn't fink she'd want dem old chairs. I was doin' her a favour."

"Those dishes," mourned Wheels. "*Vrrrmm!* They just seemed to break themselves. I hardly touched them, honest."

"No need for her to lose her temper like that though," said Twinge. "All those sparks. Brrr."

"Next time, I don't think it should be cleaning," sighed Shy. "I think it should be something else."

6. The Dwarf

"Yes?" said the Dwarf with the gardening shears. His name was Arthur Greenmangle and he had a tiny, perfect garden. He stood on a

wobbly ladder, all set to trim
the two glorious cherry trees
which stood on either side of his
gate. The gate had a sign on it:

Two Trees
Cottage

Arthur had spent the entire
morning digging, weeding, mowing

and raking. The only thing left to do was to trim the cherry trees to an equal height. The one on the left was slightly taller. It was a job he always put off because, like most Dwarfs, he didn't like heights.

"Need any help, mister?" said Cloreen. "Dig your garden? Mow the grass?"

"Any gardening experience?" asked Arthur Greenmangle. He frowned down at the Goblineers, clutching the ladder and wobbling horribly.

"No," said Oggy.

"But we're willing to learn," added Shy shyly. "We just want to do a good deed."

"For instance, I could do dat for you," offered Tuf. "Den you wouldn't have to stand on de ladder …"

A short while later, the Goblineers
were back in the Club House. Again.

"I kept telling you," said Twinge
bitterly. "I kept saying you were
taking too much off the first one."

"I didn't mean to," said Tuf sadly.

"My arm slipped. Den I had to make de udder one match. An' den – an' den dat one was too short, an' everyone was shoutin' an' …"

"It's all right," said Shy, patting his friend's knee. "We know what happened. We saw. Don't think about it any more."

"Mr Greenmangle wasn't very happy, was he?" sighed Wheels.

"He'll have to change the sign to
Two Stumps Cottage."

"That's the second good deed that
went wrong," said Cloreen. "Now
what shall we do?"

"No more gardenin', dat's for
sure," said Tuf.

7. The Nice Old Lady

The nice little old lady stood by the bus stop in the lane, waiting for the Number Seven Bus to take her to Goblin Town. She was taking a basket full of brown eggs to market.

The one thing she *didn't* want to do
was cross the road.

She sniffed and looked the other
way when the Goblineers came up.
Goblins in Gaggles usually spelled
trouble. To her dismay, the pigtailed
one in the pink hat reached out and
took her basket away.

"Here!" protested the old lady.

"What are you doing?"

"I'm carrying it across the road for you," explained Cloreen. "It's a good deed."

"But I ..." To the old lady's horror, the one on skates took away her walking stick and her arms were firmly gripped by two others.

"Don't you not worry," said Tuf.

"We'll get you across."

"But I don't …"

Her feet left the ground and she found herself being carried across the road, away from the bus stop, just as the bus came rumbling around the corner in a cloud of smoke. Grizzle screamed with joy. He loved the bus. Between him and the noise of the

engine, her feeble protests were
drowned out.

"There," said Cloreen, handing
back the basket. "All done."

"*Vrrrmmm!* Here's your stick," said
Wheels.

The bus drove away. Grizzle began
howling and Twinge gave him a
stone to suck.

"But I didn't want to cross the
road!" wailed the nice little old lady.
The Goblineers stared at her. Then at
each other. Then back at her again.

"You didn't?" said Tuf.

"No. I wanted the bus. I was going
to market to sell my eggs."

A silence fell.

"What'll you do with them," asked

Oggy, "now
you can't sell them?"

The nice
old lady had
a not-so-nice
gleam in her eye.
She reached into
the basket.

"This," she
said.

The sun was sinking in the sky as the
Goblineers walked through the woods
on their way home to tea. Grizzle was
fast asleep on Twinge's back.

"It's been some day," remarked
Oggy.

"Shame about the good deeds,"
said Cloreen. "But you can't say we
didn't try."

Shy said nothing. He was covered
in mud and soot. He had lost a
jumper and there was egg down his
coat. But all his dreams had come
true! He belonged to a real Gaggle.
He was a Goblineer with a proper
Club House. Best of all, his new
friend Tuf had invited him back for
tea. So what if the good deeds hadn't

worked out? There was always
tomorrow.

Right now, he was the happiest
Goblin in the world. Or he would be,
if only there were sausages for tea.

There were too.